For Anna, Claire and Mom

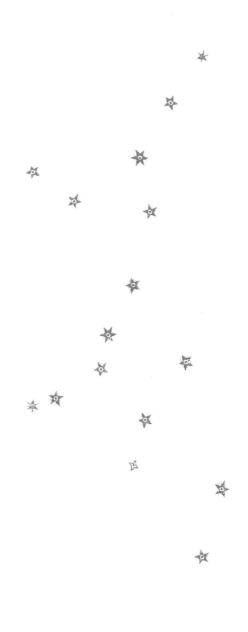

Once upon a time, about 4 and a half billion years ago...

...in the outer spiral arm of one of
billions of galaxies...

...a planet was born.

No one knew at the time that this particular planet would grow to the ripe old age of about 10 billion years before dying.

(And possibly being cremated at the same time.)

After a period of a few billion years,
when it was well into middle age,
the planet was able to sustain life,
and so it did.

It sustained many different kinds
of life.

Which gradually led to human life.

When humans first lived on the planet, they only lasted 20-30 years, or .00000550660792951542 percent of the age of the planet.

But as time went on and they discovered things and learned how to take care of themselves, they began to live longer and longer, increasing their lifespan to 70-80 years.

Still, that was only .00000165198237 percent of the age of their home.

Most adult humans were between
five and six feet tall.

And on a planet that's almost
8000 miles in diameter, that height
proved to be a bit disorienting.

Since it was too vast for a tiny human to see its rounded sides, humans believed that the planet was flat.

It seemed like a big disk. If they wandered too far, they might fall right off.

So, when they saw the horizon, they assumed it was a precarious edge.

Much later, the more exploratory humans learned how to sail boats and make machines that could fly, and they gradually learned that they lived on a globe.

And even later, when they could travel to its moon, they would bring back photographic evidence that when it was compared to the stars and nearby planets, it was just a tiny ball, somehow suspended all alone in the vast blackness of space.

But in this story, we're not there yet.

We're on a day, long before that, when a human first asked the question...

"Why?"

Why this particular group of humans on this particular rock in this particular spot in space at this particular time?

That's a big question that has been pondered for almost as long as there have been humans, which is really just .0055066079 percent of the current age of the planet.

When humans have questions, they like to answer those questions as soon as possible.

A question without an answer is always in danger of becoming a *nagging* question.

So, humans began to answer their questions.

Without empirical proof and knowledge, all the humans had were beliefs.

Some put forth the belief that a great, benevolent Supreme Being had placed them all on this little round ball, and that they were in fact that Being's *chosen* ones.

And further, if they lived well they would be rewarded with a life in the sky, away from the hardships and struggle of life on the surface of the planet.

And for those who believed, that answer felt right and comforting.

But across the great expanses
of land, or the even greater expanses
of oceans, other humans believed
that a different Supreme Being had
placed them on the planet and that
they were the chosen ones.

And their answer felt right and
comforting to *them*.

One might surmise that humans
were satisfied with their answers.
And they were.

But soon, their strong beliefs made
one set of humans *certain* that the
other set of humans had to
be wrong.

Heck, they were worse than that.

They were said to be heathens or savages or unbelievers, even though in many cases one group of humans was not even aware of exactly what the other humans believed.

And as they became more and more aware of each other's beliefs, it began to seem that each group's Supreme Being somehow authorized his or her chosen ones to slaughter the chosen ones of the other Supreme Being(s).

Meanwhile, another group of
humans looked at how the sky was
awfully big, and wondered what
lay beyond it.

Gradually they realized that it
quickly became black space.

And they thought that if they were floating in that black space, perhaps they would find that it held other worlds...maybe even *billions* of other worlds like this one existed somewhere in this universe.

Or maybe even billions of other *universes.*

And these humans wondered why a Supreme Being would choose this one tiny planet, and further why *multiple* Supreme Beings would choose this one tiny planet and then cram it full of their various chosen ones?

This question didn't necessarily have an answer. But it did lead them to question the belief in a Supreme Being. And soon, for some, to question a belief in *any Supreme Being.*

And that led to the supposition that maybe there were no Supreme Beings at all.

That maybe all the people on this tiny ball in space came to be "chosen" by nothing but the randomness of nature.

This theory was *based* on the observable randomness of nature.

And it felt right and comforting to those who theorized it.

Meanwhile, the different groups of chosen ones around the tiny planetary ball spinning in vast, empty space were building monuments to their Supreme Beings.

They created amazing art and beautiful music and stunning, impressive architecture.

Since each Supreme Being's chosen
people had different interpretations
of their particular Supreme Being,
there ended up being many
different styles of art, music
and architecture.

Each style was beautiful and familiar to some, while others found it strange. And, even at times, offensive.

These opinions depended on where a particular human stood on the planet and in which Supreme Being they believed.

Sometimes humans were united
by more than just their belief in a
Supreme Being.

Sometimes, the skin color of
humans united them.

These humans tended to stay in groups with others that looked like them, and they would fight or shun the ones who looked different.

There were some (who had previously contemplated the randomness of nature) who pointed out that beneath that skin, no matter its color, humans were *exactly* the same.

But that fact, for some reason, was not very popular (or perhaps as easily observed, except during the aftermath of battle...or in books).

Undaunted, those humans that studied the randomness of nature began to study the building blocks of nature.

They discovered that not only were humans exactly the same under their skin, but that nature (as far as they could observe, which would extend farther and farther into space), and indeed the universe, were made of identical building blocks.

These discoveries gradually led to inventions of machines that could carry people across the water, and later through the skies.

When the humans began to travel greater distances, they also began to relocate to different parts of the planet to live. And their different skin colors slowly began to mix.

And more and more humans began to notice that all humans were humans. They simply came from different parts of this tiny planet, spinning all alone in the vast blackness of space.

Still, some humans clung to the thought that their skin color was the best color, and they continued to shun or ridicule or hate those that didn't look like them.

And then one day, a child was born.

It doesn't matter where on the tiny planet the child was born, or even what gender the child was.

In fact, there were over 350,000 children born all over the planet that same day.

But we'll single out this child for one simple reason. This child grew up to ponder anew the questions that for so long had been asked and answered.

As this human child grew and learned and studied the history of its tiny planet, and examined all the times that different groups of chosen people had fought other groups of chosen people because they believed their Supreme Being was more Supreme than other Supreme Beings, the child began to have questions.

Questions with no readily available answers.

Nagging questions.

And as the human child studied
each of the religions that were built
around the beliefs in Supreme
Beings, the child began to see
similarities in their art and music
and architecture, and in their stories
and parables and philosophies.

Which led to *more* questions.

Some of those questions began
with "Why?".

And many began with "What if...?".

Why did humans feel like they needed to answer the question of *why* they were on this planet?

And *what if* humans were simply looking for more meaning in their lives, and that over time they'd developed these beliefs to provide that meaning?

And *why* wouldn't they want meaning?

After all, being born onto a tiny spinning ball in the vast and lonely blackness of space is a daunting proposition.

Especially when this human child considered that under the very best of circumstances, no human on the planet would live to be more than .0000024229075 percent of the age of the planet.

Which led to *more* questions.

What if that short time on the planet was the *reason* humans wanted and needed more meaning?

Which led the human child to study
what other groups of humans
believed about the *end* of
the planet.

In the "randomness of nature"
camp, it was theorized that the end
would come in about 1.5 billion
more years.

That's about the time that no more
humans would be able to live on the
planet, anyway. And that seemed
like a good measure of the life of
the planet, especially to the child.

Knowing what the child knew about the current age of the planet meant that metaphorically, if the planet was a human who would live to be 100, it was already 75 years old.

It was entering old age.

The old, lifeless planet would
dodder around in its dotage for a
few billion more years, at which
time the star that had warmed the
planet for many billions of years,
and helped it to support life, would
grow from what was called
a "yellow dwarf" to what was
called a "red giant."

It would expand so much that the 93 million miles that currently separated it from the planet would be filled with its giganticness.

And even if it never engulfed the planet, its heat would incinerate any evidence of the history and legacies of every human who ever walked it.

Including this very short book.

It would basically end the life of the planet and possibly cremate it at the same time.

Well, not precisely in the same moment, but perhaps in the same "geological moment."

And that would be the end of
the planet.

No philosophical differences about
Supreme Beings would continue
after that.

Nor would any scientific conclusions
based on the randomness of nature.

Each of the humans who followed their particular Supreme Beings had stories about the end of time, too.

Many of those stories were about death and destruction of the unbelievers.

Some even included the miraculous saving of the people who truly believed in the *correct* Supreme Being.

Finally, the human child was left with many possible answers to the nagging question of "What happens at the end?"

And, as we've established earlier, humans want answers to their questions.

But this human child said, "If we're all going to die...and from the planet's perspective we're all going to die very *soon* because we only live for a tiny percentage of its own life, then maybe I'm good with unanswered questions...

...maybe a *nagging* question doesn't need an answer. Maybe instead of looking at it as an unanswerable question...

I'll call it an unsolvable mystery."

And instead of trying to solve that
unsolvable mystery, the grownup
child decided to be fascinated by it.

And do the math.

If the child's expected life span
on the planet was 70-80 years, or
.00000165198237 percent of the
planet's life, that child was only
alive for a blip.

And that meant that every human, who was exactly the same under their skin, and regardless of which Supreme Being (or no Supreme Being) they believed in, would also spend only a blip on the planet.

And somehow, the unsolvable
mystery and the realization of that
blip brought comfort to that
grownup child.

And led to one question...

A question that would have a unique answer for each individual human who decided to ask it...

How do I make the most of my blip?

With gratitude and love to my wife Anna, who helped me look so differently at the world, and whom I'll love long after my blip (and long after the Earth's blip, too!). To my daughter Claire, who's made me wish for a much longer blip, and whose perspective is (and will be) a gift to the hearts and minds of humans everywhere. To the fine emergency doctors in New Orleans who helped make sure I got to live my blip to its full potential. To Bard Richmond, whose scientific mind and musical sensibility has always inspired me to do the math (or ask him to!), and to Tom Schworer for his finely honed editor and design eyes (and skills). To Anna's grandmother, whose blip extended to 105 years, and who would say to the Earth, as she said to my Mother, "Oh, honey...you're just getting started on old age at 75." And to my mother, who thankfully spent some of her blip raising me. Also, to the crew of Apollo 8, who first took those spectacular pictures of Earth from the Moon and made me think, in my naïve youth, "Hey...we're all alone out here. Once everybody sees these pictures, there'll be no more wars!"